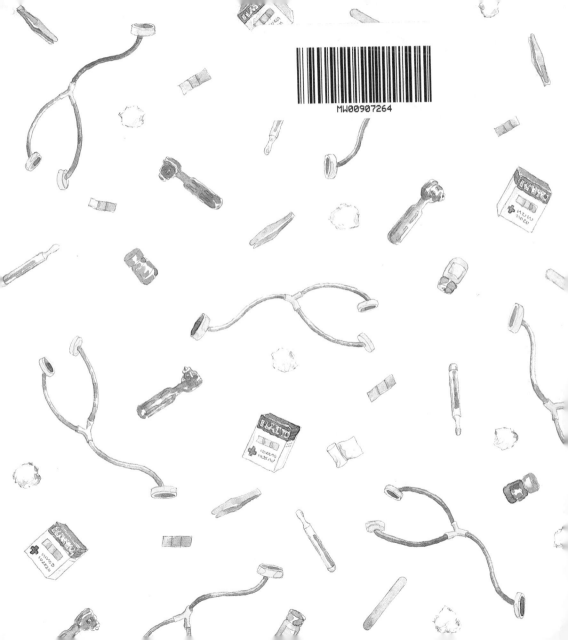

For Wendy

VIKING KESTREL
Viking Penguin Inc.,
40 West 23rd Street,
New York, New York 10010, U.S.A.

First published in Great Britain by Walker Books Ltd 1986
First American Edition   Published in 1986
Copyright © Niki Daly, 1986
All rights reserved   Printed in Italy
1   2   3   4   5   90   89   88   87   86

Library of Congress catalog card number: 86-40020
(CIP data available)
ISBN 0-670-81254-4

Thank You Henrietta

Niki Daly

Viking Kestrel

Henrietta liked to help
around the house.

When there were dishes to wash,
Henrietta washed and Dad dried.

When Mom needed somebody small,
Henrietta always lent a hand.

One day Mom's washing-
machine wouldn't work.
It went *click-click*.
"It should go *glug-glug*,"
Mom complained.

Dad got his tool-box.
Henrietta brought
her hammer.

Dad pushed and twisted with
the screwdriver.
Henrietta tapped and banged
with her hammer.
"Ouch!" yelled Dad.
The screwdriver had slipped
and cut his finger.

Dad sat and watched his
finger bleed.
"Don't cry, Dad," said
Henrietta. And she ran
to her room.

Henrietta came back with
her first-aid kit. She
opened it and took out
her doctor's things.
Mom brought the bandaids.

Henrietta took Dad's temperature.
Then she listened to his heartbeat.
"I think Dad needs a bandaid,"
said Mom.

Henrietta put the bandaid
on Dad's finger.
"Thank you, Henrietta," said Dad.

Then Dad fixed the
washing-machine.
Ping went the button.
Glug-glug went the machine.
When the wash was done,
Mom hung it out to dry
all by herself.

Henrietta was too tired to help.

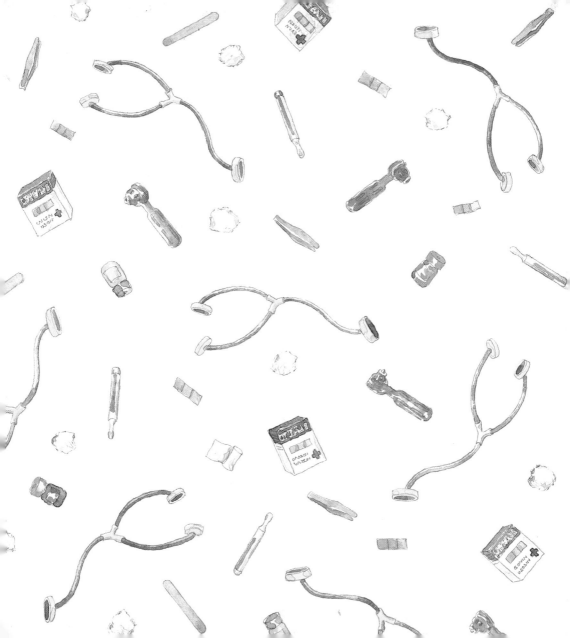